THE IKUN SHIP

Written by Elen Caldecott

Illustrated by Alessia Trunfio

Words to look out for ...

collective (*adjective*)
A collective action or decision is done or shared by the members of a group.

complex (*adjective*)
Complex means complicated or difficult, because of having a lot of different parts.

defend (*verb*)
defends, defending, defended
To defend someone or something is to protect them from an attack.

discriminate (*verb*)
discriminates, discriminating, discriminated
To discriminate between things is to notice or show the differences between them.

intensive (*adjective*)
Intensive activity involves a lot of effort over a short time.

interpret (*verb*)
interprets, interpreting, interpreted
To interpret something is to explain or understand what it means.

obsess (*verb*)
obsesses, obsessing, obsessed
To be obsessed with something, or to obsess over something, is to be continually thinking about it.

progress (*noun*)
To make progress is to become better, or to make something better.

strategy (*noun*)
A strategy is a plan to achieve something.

sufficient (*adjective*)
enough

Introducing ...

Noa Goodwin

Ada Goodwin

Dr Bran Goodwin

Renwick

Dr Edwin Grimes

3

Prologue

Noa gripped the Never Door handle and turned it. A cold mist streamed out as the door swung open. Through the pitch-black, Noa saw the lights of the time tunnel swirling in the distance. A furious cry broke out behind her, and Renwick squawked an urgent warning. Noa spun round as Grimes skidded across the broad desk, scattering her dad's papers, and ran towards the Never Door.

He lunged for her with his arms outstretched. Noa jumped into the time tunnel, Renwick clinging to her shoulder. She felt wind start to swirl all around, twisting her hair and buffeting her cheeks. She had forgotten how all-encompassing the darkness was inside the tunnel, how it seemed to stretch away endlessly. But there was no time to wonder at it all. She had to stop Grimes from following her before the time tunnel pulled her away. Already the wind was rising; she didn't have long. Noa tried to close the door behind her, pushing at it with all her might.

Then, she felt Grimes' weight slam into the wood. She was thrown back into the time tunnel. The Never Door was flung open.

Grimes stumbled over the threshold, panting. He stared at the key in Noa's hand. Noa gripped it tighter, knowing how much Grimes wanted it.

Grimes leapt forward. She feinted left. He charged left. She ducked right. They danced around each other as they stepped further and further into the tunnel. The wind howled, and Noa felt Renwick's claws grip her shoulder fiercely. She could feel herself being lifted up by the wind: her feet barely touched the ground. Lights pulsed pink and blue and purple. The tunnel was about to pull them both back in time.

'Give me the key, Noa,' Grimes growled.

'It's mine. Dad left it for me,' Noa said defiantly.

'And where is your dad, exactly?' Grimes asked.

A lump formed in her throat. She didn't know where her dad was. He had been gone such a long time. Her eyes blurred.

'Kwarrk!' Renwick cawed wildly.

His cry snapped Noa to attention, but it came too late. While she was momentarily distracted, Grimes seized his chance. He lurched forward and grabbed the key from her hand.

'No!' cried Noa, clutching at thin air.

Grimes raised the Never Door key in triumph. 'Finally!' he said gleefully. 'The key is mine!'

It was then that the full force of the time tunnel was unleashed. The wind barrelled into them, scooping them up as though they were made of feathers. The power of it knocked Renwick from Noa's shoulder, but he beat his strong wings and glided through the air. She tried to keep sight of Grimes, but it was hard to tell which way was up as they were dragged forward.

Noa caught flashes of side tunnels, dozens of possible routes into history. She thought she heard Grimes yelling, but the wind was so loud she couldn't be sure.

Then the wind died, and she landed in a heap on the ground. She shook her head to clear the ringing noise.

'Renwick! Are you all right?' she asked. He cawed softly: he was safe. Grimes was on his feet already. He stood in front of a dark metal door; the enormous iron slab was set with brass cogs and an elaborately decorated keyhole. Small puffs of smoke came through vents set in the metal. Grimes slotted the key into the lock and reached for the brass handle. Noa scrambled to stand.

'Kwarrk!' Renwick squawked urgently.

Grimes opened the door.

If Grimes made it through, then the key might be lost forever. And, along with it, all hope of being able to get home or find her dad.

With a last mean look back at her, Grimes stepped through the doorway.

Noa ignored the heat from the steaming vents and crawled towards the closing door.

Chapter 1

Noa's day had not started with a chase through the Never Door. It had begun perfectly normally.

She had spent the morning in intensive study – reading a fascinating book on the science of space travel from cover to cover. In the afternoon she had helped Aunt Ada in the museum; it seemed that as soon as they finished dusting the last case in the gallery it was almost time to start again, but Aunt Ada called for a break. Then, for a little while, Noa and Renwick had worked on their tricks – Noa had taught him to fetch items using a special signal. She would look at Renwick, point at the object, then tap her finger three times on her leg, and he would bring it to her.

The museum was an enormous room, piled high with shelves and display cases, with a balcony running all the way around the top – it was full of secret, shadow-filled spots that were perfect for playing hide and seek when she was little. She thought of those times fondly; her mum would

Intensive activity involves a lot of effort over a short time.

most often be buried in her books, researching each curiosity in the museum. Dad would probably be sorting through deliveries or scribbling in his notebook. The museum would always make her think of her parents first and foremost. They could tell Noa the story of every single item in it. She loved imagining the lives of the people who had used the items. Now, Aunt Ada managed the museum since Mum was gone and Dad was away.

Aunt Ada thought Dad was travelling for business, but Noa suspected he had journeyed through the Never Door. Aunt Ada didn't know about the Never Door and Noa had no intention of telling her. Her aunt had to keep the museum going, which was enough to worry about.

Ever since she had found the stained-glass window in the attic, Noa had become more and more certain Dad had gone in search of her mum, but it had been weeks since she last saw him. She was so worried; she couldn't lose him too …

'Kwarrk! Kwarrk!' Renwick squawked. He flew down from a case that displayed a collection of

musical boxes and landed on the ground beside Noa. He always knew when she was feeling down.

She reached out gently and stroked his gleaming black feathers.

'Kwarrk!' he said again, a little more softly.

'I know. Dad will be alright,' Noa told Renwick. She wished she felt as certain as she sounded. 'I just wish he'd come home, that's all.'

She dangled her legs over the balcony edge, looking round at the curated collections. She knew them all so well, but never got bored staring at them. Even the old Victorian display cases were beautiful, their woodwork ornately carved with leaves and flower designs, though they were scuffed and chipped in places now.

Turning her head to look over at Renwick, something small caught Noa's eye, underneath the nearest case – a single penny that someone had dropped accidentally.

'See a penny, pick it up, all that day you'll have good luck,' she muttered. It was something Dad had said sometimes when she was little. She could

do with a little good luck. She reached her arm under the display case and grabbed the penny. She slipped it in her pocket and hoped today would be the day that Dad returned.

'Noa? Where are you, dear?' Aunt Ada called.

Noa got up and brushed herself down.

'Noa?'

'Coming, Aunt Ada,' Noa replied.

As she crossed the gallery, she couldn't help but notice that it was looking a little tired, a little shabby. The handle had fallen off one of the cabinets, and another had a cracked pane of glass. There hadn't been enough visitors lately, so there wasn't money to spend on repairs. *No wonder Aunt Ada is so worried*, Noa thought. But her aunt hid it well.

Aunt Ada was standing in the entrance hall, at the neat little information desk that greeted anyone who visited. It displayed a plan of the museum, and some folding maps that visitors could carry around with them. It also had a money till on it, a till that Noa knew was mostly empty.

'There you are!' Aunt Ada said. She was grinning. 'I sold three tickets today, isn't that wonderful?'

Three tickets were better than no tickets, Noa supposed. 'Yes, Aunt Ada.'

'I'm going to make us tea and biscuits to celebrate. Would you mind watching the museum for me, dear? In case our visitors need any help?'

Noa nodded. Back in the main gallery, she spotted the visitors. A couple stood near the Victorian fashion display, happily talking to each other and pointing out their favourite clothes. Near the antique doll display, a young woman sketched in a notebook.

Noa was about to return to the information desk when she spotted another figure. At the other end of the gallery, a man peered into the display of clocks and watches. He was tall, and had blonde hair slicked with gel. He wore a dark suit. Though he stood with his back to Noa, there was something about him that made her feel very uneasy. How had he got into the museum?

Noa wandered closer. She stopped near the

display of ceramic teapots and took out a polishing cloth from her pockets. As she shone the glass, she watched the man in the reflection.

The man turned. As soon as she saw his face, she recognized him – Dr Edwin Grimes. Renwick cawed fretfully.

What was he doing here? The last time she'd seen him, he'd demanded money from Aunt Ada, saying Dad owed him. Admittedly she had been eavesdropping at the time and perhaps shouldn't have listened in. But now she was glad that she had. Had he come to make trouble again? She rubbed the already shining glass cabinet, so she could continue to watch him.

Grimes stepped towards her, past the display of kettles and early computers.

'Good afternoon,' he said.

Noa was forced to turn and nod her head.

'Kwarrk!' Renwick crowed.

'Ah, *that* bird. An interesting choice of pet,' he said, smiling as though it were painful. 'This whole museum is remarkably interesting. Remarkably.'

'Thank you,' Noa replied. She remembered the job Aunt Ada had given her. 'Do you need help finding anything in particular?'

Grimes eyes widened. Maybe he wasn't expecting her to be so welcoming. He patted down his waistcoat. 'It's Noa, isn't it? You won't remember me, but I knew your parents, a long time ago. We were at university together.'

'Really?' Noa said. 'So, you were friends?' Dad had never mentioned Grimes, but she had seen a photograph of him once, on Dad's desk.

'Yes,' Grimes replied, but he didn't sound very convincing. 'How is your father? Doing well, I hope?'

Why was he being so nice? Last time he had visited he hadn't been at all friendly. 'Dad's fine,' she said, hoping it was true.

'Last time we spoke, Bran told me he was working on something that we'd talked about as students.'

The breath caught in Noa's throat. When had Grimes spoken to Dad? Recently? 'When was that?' Noa asked cautiously.

'Oh, a good while ago now,' he said, with a casual wave of his hand. Then his eyes sharpened. 'I expect he's made a lot of progress since then. I was hoping to catch up with him about it, actually. Is he here?'

Noa didn't reply. She looked away and tried to hide her disappointment from Grimes.

'Ah,' Grimes said, seeing the look on her face. 'I'm sorry to have missed him. It's never quite the right *time*, it seems.'

Noa gave a small start. Why had Grimes said it like that? Renwick shuffled uncomfortably on her shoulder; she knew that he didn't like Grimes very much either. 'Were you and my dad in the same university classes then?' Noa asked, hoping to glean some information about him.

'We studied physics together under Professor Shaw. She was a brilliant scholar. Your mother was at university with us too. Such a sad loss. After graduation, I invested in your father's research. I wonder, does he have a workshop here, a laboratory, perhaps? I'd be very curious to take

---

To make progress is to become better, or to make something better.

a quick look, for old times' sake, you understand. He was always so gifted. So talented.'

Noa gave a quick smile, despite her misgivings. Dad *was* gifted. He *was* talented. He worked so hard, too. He'd been able to invent the Never Door and find a way to travel through time!

'Perhaps he keeps an outbuilding or shed for his experiments?' Grimes continued.

'He just has his study,' Noa said. 'But I don't think he'd like it if I showed it to you.'

He held up both hands in apology. 'I'm so sorry, I didn't mean to put you on the spot. Your father must have given you very strict instructions not to reveal the location of the Time Door.'

'What? No! I mean ... I don't know what you're talking about,' Noa said hurriedly. She clamped her lips together. She shouldn't say another word.

Grimes clapped his hands in delight. 'Oh, Noa! Thank you so much for this marvellous news.'

'But I didn't give you any news!' Noa exclaimed.

It seemed that Grimes wasn't listening to her any more. His eyes darted around the museum, landing

on every door and window and cupboard.

'Well, well, well, Bran Goodwin, you only went and did it …' Grimes said wistfully.

Oh no! What had she done?

'Noa, dear. Is everything alright?' Aunt Ada's voice came like a welcome hug. Noa relaxed her shoulders a little. Crossing the gallery space, Aunt Ada carried a silver tea tray, set with two delicate cups and a small plate of the good biscuits.

Grimes looked over at Aunt Ada, whose face was stern. It was clear she recognized Grimes straight away. 'Ah, Ms Goodwin. How wonderful to see you again. Your niece has been so, so helpful. But it was high *time* I was off.' He gave Noa a small bow that made her tummy squirm. 'Thank you, this visit has been most enlightening.'

Noa watched Grimes head towards the exit. As he walked, she fretted over every word she'd said.

———•⚷•———

Grimes crossed the gallery floor. That girl had given him such a tantalizing clue. He could tell immediately that she was lying. He was getting close, so close he could almost taste it! Bran wasn't here the last time he had visited and still wasn't. Clearly, he'd been gone for a while. And the child had all but admitted that the Time Door was real, which meant the key to use it must be too. Bran must have taken the money that he, Grimes, had invested and travelled in time himself.

Glee turned quickly to resentment. It wasn't fair. He had put all that money into Bran's research and for what? He hadn't made a single penny. He was about to head out into the street, when an idea struck him.

He glanced back. Noa and her aunt were out of sight. Gone to drink their tea, no doubt. The gallery was full of nooks and crannies, dark gloomy places where someone might hide until the coast was clear ... Where someone might wait, then sneak out after nightfall to search this place from top to bottom.

Smiling to himself, Grimes slid between an old dressing table and a wall tapestry, crouched down and waited.

Chapter 2

Grimes waited in the shadows until Ada rang the bell for closing time. He heard her wish a good evening to the few visitors who were still there. He stayed silent, motionless, as she closed the front door. He lingered in his hiding place until she turned off the lights and the museum plunged into darkness.

The sound of Ada and Noa's voices grew quieter as they went through the door that joined their house to the museum. He risked pulling out his phone, to use its torch. The vast space was his to explore. He would take his time, looking behind every object and inside every cupboard … he would find the Time Door and the key to unlock it before the night was over.

Noa and Aunt Ada had a supper of cheese on toast in the small sitting room. Noa enjoyed these quiet evenings with her aunt, cosied up on the sofa, watching movies or playing board games.

Much like the museum, the house had become a bit shabby but it was still *home*.

Noa's favourite room was her dad's study. She wasn't supposed to go in there without him, but she found herself drawn to it in his absence. It contained all her dad's research and books and, of course, the Never Door – the door she was never to use. When her dad was home, she was only allowed in the study occasionally. At those times, she would sit by the fireplace while he told her stories from the past, tales of ancient Egypt or the advancements of the Industrial Revolution … stories that felt so real, it was almost as if he'd been there to see it.

Noa lifted a crust from her plate and let Renwick peck at it delightedly. If only she could hear one of Dad's stories tonight.

'Aunt Ada,' she asked sadly. 'Have you heard from Dad at all?'

Aunt Ada frowned. She put her plate down on a side table. 'No, sorry, my darling. He said he might be out of contact for a while.' Aunt Ada's hands twitched in her lap. 'Somewhere without phone signal. I'm sure he's making great progress, raising money from investors or finding a new exhibit that will have visitors rushing through our door.'

Noa had her own suspicions of where Bran was, but she didn't want to worry Aunt Ada any further.

'He'll come home as soon as he can, I know it,' Aunt Ada continued, 'and when he does come back, the museum will be restored.'

Noa took their empty plates through to the kitchen. She didn't like the fact that Grimes had come to the museum today. It felt wrong. It felt dangerous. The sooner Dad came home the better.

————— •⚷• —————

Grimes was furious.

He had looked over every single inch of the public gallery, from the tiled floor to the balcony above and there was no sign at all of the Time Door. He had found every other kind of curiosity – from teddy bears to Turkish bathtubs, the museum had amazing artefacts from different periods in history. But the Time Door wasn't here.

To make progress is to become better, or to make something better.

He was sweaty and dusty and tired, but he wasn't ready to give up. There was one place left to look. That child, Noa, had mentioned a study. He had assumed it would be in the museum, close to all the other curiosities, but perhaps it was in their house.

He would need to get Ada Goodwin and that annoying girl out of the way.

He cast his eyes around the gallery and the objects it housed from all over the world. As he took in all the items, an idea began to form. He knew how he could get them out of the building. It was perfect!

He unlocked his phone and cleared his throat. He would need to disguise his voice. 'Good evening,' he practised in his most high-pitched voice. No, that was too squeaky.

He tried again, this time in his lowest voice, 'Good evening.' That was better, he sounded mysterious and not at all like himself.

Grimes tapped his phone.

———— • ✺ • ————

Noa and Aunt Ada's conversation was interrupted by the sound of the phone ringing.

Noa felt her heart lift, just a fraction – could it be Dad?

Aunt Ada rose and picked up the phone on the writing desk. 'Hello? Good evening.'

There was a pause, then Aunt Ada said, 'I see … yes … now? OK … we should be there in about twenty minutes. Thank you for letting me know.'

Noa's pulse quickened. Was Dad in trouble? As soon as Aunt Ada put the phone down, Noa asked, 'What is it? What's wrong?'

Aunt Ada shook her head. 'Oh, don't worry, dear. There's simply a new delivery for the museum. It just arrived at the depot, but apparently there's a problem with the paperwork. I have to go and sign something before the driver will deliver it to us. Your father must have sent us something wonderful to put on display.' Aunt Ada hurried into the hall and Noa could hear her putting on her coat and boots. 'Will you come with me?' Aunt Ada called.

Dad had sent them something? Perhaps the delivery contained a letter or postcard from him, too! Noa was just about to jump up when she thought again about Grimes. This news from Dad on exactly the same day that Grimes had been nosing around the exhibits made her feel uncomfortable. Was it just a coincidence? Why had he been in the museum today? She felt cross that she had accidentally given Grimes even the smallest clue that the Never Door was real.

She knew she couldn't leave the Never Door unguarded tonight.

If Aunt Ada went out, then that would give her the perfect opportunity to go to Dad's study without having to sneak past her. Dad didn't like people going into the study without him, but Noa needed to look at the notebook again. She'd never heard her dad talk about investors in his research, only investing in the museum, but maybe she had missed something.

Noa stretched her arms up and made the biggest yawning sound that she could. 'Sorry, Aunt Ada,

I'm so tired. I don't think I should go out. I might get an early night.'

Aunt Ada's face popped into the doorway. 'Are you all right? It's still quite early.'

Noa nodded. 'I know. I'm fine. It was just a long day.' She faked another big yawn.

'All right. Well, I shan't be long. And my phone is on if you need me.'

'Good night, Aunt Ada,' Noa said.

'Good night, dear.'

Noa waited until she heard the door close, then she dashed out of her chair, up the stairs and along to Dad's study. Renwick flew beside her.

In moments, she had Dad's notebook open on the desk. Was there anything in here about Grimes? Anything at all about where Dad was and when he was coming back? She flipped the pages, but they were just lists of dates, complex equations and random sentences that she didn't understand. She glanced over at the red velvet curtain that hid the Never Door.

She had stepped through it once before and

Complex means complicated or difficult, because of having a lot of different parts.

found herself in 1910. It had been an adventure, but she hadn't found her dad.

Since then, she had pored over Dad's notebook, obsessing over how the Never Door worked, in case it could help her get him back. But it was all so complicated. *Where are you, Dad?*

'Kwarrk!'

Noa glanced up to see Renwick staring out of the window. Outside, the full moon cast milky shadows across the garden. Renwick's favourite oak tree rustled in the breeze.

'Do you want to go outside?' Noa asked. She drew up the blinds and opened the window. Renwick flew out, silent as the night.

As she moved back to the desk, she heard a noise. A door opening. It came from the hall beyond the study. Was Aunt Ada home already? That didn't seem right. Maybe she had forgotten something? Noa moved silently to the door. She crouched down and peered through the keyhole. She could just make out a man's shape in the shadows. She knew who it was at once – Grimes!

To be obsessed with something, or to obsess over something, is to be continually thinking about it.

In an instant, Noa realized she might be in danger. She scanned the room for somewhere to hide. Then she raced across the study and slipped behind the thick velvet curtain. It hid her completely. Against her back, she could feel the vibration coming from the Never Door. She was just in time. Right at that moment the study door opened.

With her heart pounding and her legs trembling, she risked a peek from behind the curtain.

Noa saw Grimes step carefully into the room. How dare he! Anger wrestled with fear as she watched him peer around the study. His gaze rested on the notebook, which she had left on the desk. *Please don't look*. Her hands moved to the Never Door key she kept in her pocket. Without thought, she nervously rolled the barrel of the key with her fingertips. If Grimes read Dad's notebook it would be her fault. She should have hidden it properly when she had the chance!

Grimes picked up the notebook. He sat down *in Dad's chair* and opened the cover.

Chapter 3

Noa could hardly believe it. Not only had Grimes broken into their house, but he had also made himself comfortable at Dad's desk and was—right now—reading through Dad's personal notebook. It was outrageous. She could feel herself shaking with rage. How dare Grimes sit at Dad's desk and relax in Dad's chair? Dad would be home *any day* now—any minute—Noa just knew it, and here was Grimes behaving like Dad was gone for good.

She wanted to rush out and confront Grimes. To shout at him to get up and get out! But, if she left her hiding place behind the curtain, she would reveal the location of the Never Door.

'Kwarrk!'

Renwick! She realized then that she wasn't alone, not while Renwick was close. She risked moving the curtain aside, just a tiny amount, to be able to see the window. Grimes was so busy at the desk, reading and muttering to himself as he scanned Dad's notes, that he didn't notice her small movement in the shadows of the study.

Renwick stood on the window ledge, watching the study. His sharp eyes picked her out straight away. Renwick would be able to help. Noa gave their special signal – she pointed at the notebook and tapped her finger on her leg three times. Renwick understood at once.

'Kwarrk! Kwarrk!' Renwick launched himself from the ledge and circled the room.

'What on earth?' Grimes dropped the notebook in surprise. He leapt to his feet. The chair tipped backwards with a clatter.

'Kwarrk!' Renwick flew at Grimes, with his wings extended, trying to look as big as he could possibly manage.

'You again!' Grimes' arms shot to cover his face. He stepped back, yelping as his shin hit the chair leg.

Renwick swerved. He landed neatly on the desk beside the dropped notebook. He hopped and picked it up smartly with his claws.

'Oh no you don't,' Grimes warned. 'I'll pluck you like a chicken!' Grimes lunged for the raven

with both arms. Renwick cawed in alarm and the notebook tumbled to the floor.

Noa squeezed her fists so tightly she could feel her nails digging into her palms. Oh Renwick!

'Come here,' Grimes growled.

Noa's breath came in shallow gasps. Grimes was trying to catch Renwick! She couldn't let him harm her best friend.

Without any further thought, Noa stepped out from behind the curtain.

Grimes, whose hands had been flailing above his head in an attempt to grab Renwick, jumped back in shock when he saw her. He howled as he banged his leg again on the chair.

'Where did you come from?' Grimes snapped. He rubbed his shin.

'I live here, if you remember,' Noa said.

Renwick flew to her shoulder. His presence boosted her confidence.

'I'm *supposed* to be here,' she continued. 'I can't say the same about you. What exactly are you doing in my dad's study?'

Grimes looked shifty, his eyes darted to the rug on the floor, to the lamp on the ceiling, as if he might find an answer to her question there.

His obvious discomfort made Noa feel a little bolder, a little braver – she was in the right, after all!

'I asked, what are you doing in my home? Why are you here?' Noa planted her hands on her hips.

She thought he wasn't going to answer, that he might just make a dash for the hallway. But he seemed to be wrestling with something himself, his face flashed with fear, then anger. 'I'm here because your dad owes me. I invested in his work and then, just as we were making progress, he snatched it all away from me. He conned me.'

What? That didn't sound like Dad. He got cross when Aunt Ada cheated at cards. He wouldn't dream of cheating on a business partner.

'That isn't true,' Noa said firmly.

Grimes banged his palm against the desk, making Noa jump. 'You don't know! You were just a baby. He had all these wonderful theories, but the

---

To make progress is to become better, or to make something better.

31

closer he got to real discoveries, the less he would tell me about it. He was <u>obsessed</u> with secrecy.'

She resisted the urge to glance back at the Never Door.

'Dad must have had his reasons,' Noa said.

Grimes bent down and retrieved the notebook from the floor. 'He wanted to shut me out! The proof is right here. Look! Lists of dates, notes about observations. He got it to work, didn't he, the Time Door?'

Noa felt a chill run through her. 'You shouldn't be reading that,' she said. 'It belongs to my dad.'

Grimes slammed the notebook onto the desk. 'This is half mine!' he insisted, pointing at it. 'I invested in the business he started. Time Share Enterprises could be a flourishing business if only he would listen to me! With access to the past, we can collect all kinds of treasures and bring them back. But no, he only cares about the science, the physics of time travel, without giving any thought to my investment. He wants to keep his invention all to himself.'

To be <u>obsessed</u> with something, or to <u>obsess</u> over something, is to be continually thinking about it.

Noa was acutely aware that the Never Door was right behind her, hidden by the velvet curtain. This was what Grimes was hunting for – that and the key in her pocket. He obviously didn't know it was here, otherwise he would have gone straight to it the second he walked in.

'He wants to keep it all,' Grimes said, almost to himself. 'Every treasure we could have discovered and brought back to auction here. Now the opportunity is gone. Lost.'

'Auction?' Had Noa heard right?

'Yes,' Grimes nodded. 'I told Bran that we could travel back in time to find Nefertiti's necklace, or Shakespeare's quill and ink, or Queen Elizabeth II's bedroom slippers … we could take anything from the past and bring it back to the present. Think how much money we'd make if we sold those things now. We'd be wealthy beyond our wildest dreams. But Bran was having none of it. As soon as I told him my plan, he froze me out. Told me he wanted no part of it.'

'Good!' Noa said. 'You can't just take things that

don't belong to you. It isn't right.'

Grimes' eyes gleamed with anger. 'You're as small-minded as your father.'

Noa felt Renwick grasp more tightly at her shoulder. He too had noticed Grimes' changed demeanour, the hardness that had settled on his face. She couldn't help but take a step back, away from him. Her palms felt the softness of the velvet curtain behind her. Gently, she drew the fabric tighter, making sure to cover every trace of the Never Door from view.

She and Renwick were the only ones standing between Grimes and all of Dad's secrets. Grimes was just a few paces away behind the desk, and it might be ages before Aunt Ada came home. She had to keep the key safe, for Dad's sake. He didn't want Grimes to have it: Grimes had said so himself. Noa calculated the distance to the hall, and the front door. Was she quick enough to dash out and through the museum to call for help?

She knew she wasn't. She looked over at the window instead. But the drop was far too high.

Noa realized there was only one place she could run. The Never Door. She didn't really know how it worked yet, so she didn't know where it would take her. But she had no choice. It was her only way out. She had the key to the door in a concealed pocket in her jacket. She always kept it close. She just had to distract Grimes long enough to be able to take it out and unlock the door.

'You know,' Noa said, 'I think I did see something about doors, or portals, or something. I thought they looked like instructions, but I didn't really understand them.'

Grimes' face lit up. 'Instructions? Where?' He glanced around the desk, at the bookshelves, and at the teetering stacks of papers and books on the floor. Bran never threw anything away, not even after he'd read it.

'It was in one of the desk drawers. I don't remember which one.'

Immediately, Grimes dived towards the drawers, tugging and pulling, struggling to open them up, because they were so jammed full of stuff.

While he was diverted, Noa moved swiftly to pull the key from her pocket.

'Where is it?' Grimes muttered, still yanking at the handles and tearing out jammed paper.

Renwick pecked gently at Noa's shoulder, urging her to hurry. She needed no encouragement. She whipped back the curtain and slipped the key into the lock. Noa gripped the Never Door handle and turned it.

A cold mist streamed out as the door swung open. Through the pitch-black, Noa saw the lights of the time tunnel swirling in the distance. A furious cry broke out behind her, and Renwick squawked an urgent warning. Noa spun round as Grimes skidded across the broad desk, scattering her dad's papers, and ran towards the Never Door.

He lunged for her with his arms outstretched. Noa jumped into the time tunnel, Renwick clinging to her shoulder. She felt wind start to swirl all around, twisting her hair and buffeting her cheeks. Noa tried to close the door behind her, pushing at it with all her might.

Then, she felt Grimes' weight slam into the wood. She was thrown back into the time tunnel. The Never Door was flung open.

Grimes stumbled over the threshold, panting. He stared at the key in Noa's hand. Noa gripped it tighter, knowing how much Grimes wanted it.

The wind howled, and Noa felt Renwick grip her shoulder fiercely. She could feel herself being lifted up: her feet barely touched the ground. The tunnel was about to pull them both back in time.

'Give me the key, Noa,' Grimes growled.

'It's mine. Dad left it for me,' Noa said defiantly.

'And where is your dad, exactly?' Grimes asked.

A lump formed in her throat. She didn't know where her dad was. He had been gone such a long time now. Her eyes blurred.

'Kwarrk!' Renwick cawed wildly.

His cry snapped Noa to attention, but it came too late. While Noa was momentarily distracted, Grimes seized his chance. He lurched forward and grabbed the key from her hand.

'No!' cried Noa, clutching at thin air.

It was then that the full force of the time tunnel was unleashed. The wind barrelled into them, scooping them up as though they were made of feathers. The power knocked Renwick from Noa's shoulder, but he beat his strong wings and glided through the air.

Noa caught flashes of side tunnels, dozens of possible routes into history. She thought she heard Grimes yelling, but the wind was so loud she couldn't be sure.

Then, the wind died, and she landed in a heap on the ground. Grimes was on his feet already. He stood in front of an enormous iron door, set with brass cogs and an elaborately decorated keyhole. Grimes slotted the key into the lock and opened the door.

If Grimes made it through, then the key might be lost forever. And, along with it, all hope of being able to get home or find her dad.

With a last mean look back at her, Grimes stepped through the doorway.

Noa scrambled towards the closing door.

Chapter 4

Grimes held the key close to his chest, in a tight grip. He staggered a little as his feet found firm ground. He had done it. Finally! *Finally!* The key to the Time Door was his. His grin stretched from ear to ear as he pocketed the precious key. *Fame and fortune, here I come!* he thought.

He took a deep breath. The air tasted of damp and soot. He looked around. Where had the door brought him? He was standing, he saw, outside a dark brick building. There was a wet, cobbled courtyard in front of him, with wooden barrels stacked in a careful pyramid to his left.

He stepped closer to them; might there be something valuable inside the barrels? Distracted, he left the door ajar behind him.

He ran his fingers over the rough surface of the wood. Each barrel seemed to be sealed tightly. There was no easy way to get inside. He looked around the courtyard: perhaps there were valuables elsewhere? The yard was small, perhaps ten metres square. There were buildings on three sides and the fourth was open to a canal or river cutting in front. Boats bobbed on the water and he could see dockworkers tugging at ropes. Nothing valuable.

'Kwarrk!'

Grimes recognized the sound in an instant. It was that annoying bird, no doubt with Noa too. They were coming through the open door. He should have slammed it shut behind him. He stepped behind the barrels and crouched. There was nothing worth taking here. He would wait until the coast was clear, then slip away to keep hunting.

'Kwarrk!' Renwick cawed, as Noa stumbled through the iron door and into bright light. It took a few moments for her senses to adjust. Her ears were filled with clangs and bangs, and shrieks, like gulls at the seaside. Her eyes were dazzled by sparks and darts of light. The air smelled of salt and spices. 'Where are we?'

She blinked and rubbed her eyes. This was the

second time she had travelled through the time tunnel, and it wasn't something she thought she would ever get used to.

As she looked around, she slowly realized that she was standing on a narrow strip of ground, between high warehouses on three sides and a broad canal of deep-looking water on the other. Past a pile of storage barrels, ships with wooden hulls and furled sails bobbed up and down on the water. Their bells clanked as the boats bumped against the canal wall. Sailors and stevedores clambered over their decks, loading and unloading their cargo.

They were at a port.

Behind her, the iron door slammed shut as though pulled by the ferocious winds inside.

'We have to find Grimes and get the key back,' she told Renwick.

Renwick cawed in agreement.

Noa crossed the courtyard and looked the dockside up and down. There were people, lots of them, scurrying in all directions. Sailors

called to each other from the ships; on land the dockworkers moved goods and trundled carts; stallholders yelled their wares: food, drinks, newspapers and more. She'd been through King's Cross Railway Station on trips outside London with Dad, but this port was even busier than that.

She looked among the crowds of people but couldn't see Grimes.

'We've lost him,' Noa said, her shoulders sinking.

Grimes had the key to the Never Door. Without it, there was no way back to the museum and no way to search for Dad. Noa had to find it – there was no alternative.

———————•🗝•———————

Grimes crouched behind the barrels. He was getting stiff legs. 'Go on, go away,' he whispered at Noa and Renwick.

She would be looking for him, of course. He had the key she needed to get home. He smiled again. She hadn't found him yet!

He peered out at the scene. Noa and her bird were like shop dummies, staring around them.

Grimes started to notice the clothes that passers-by were wearing: the dark suits and brass buttons of the clerks on the quay; the cotton and linen tunics of the sailors; he guessed he had arrived in the mid-19th century sometime. The era when Queen Victoria was on the throne. An age of invention.

Then, he saw something that made him squeal like a mouse with its tail caught in a door. It was a man, in a suit as dark as night, with a tall hat the size and shape of a black chimney pot. The man walked the dockside, deep in thought, with one hand in his waistcoat pocket. In his free hand, he carried a notebook, which he was studying intently.

He was barely looking where he walked. He was a man that Grimes recognized from a hundred paintings and portraits. It was the famous engineer, Isambard Kingdom Brunel.

'That notebook would be worth a small fortune,' Grimes said, and squealed again.

If only he wasn't stuck behind these barrels! Was that annoying child ever going to leave? She and the raven were still dithering on the dockside.

'Go away,' he muttered frustratedly. She couldn't stand there forever. She would have to leave sometime. Still, he couldn't take any chances. He would have to make sure she didn't follow him back into the tunnel … but how?

The air rang with the clamorous sounds of industry. Coming from inside the brick buildings, he could hear hammers hitting anvils, and the crackle of furnaces. Grimes smirked. A strategy was beginning to form. 'All I need is a locksmith …' he said.

He backed cautiously towards a wooden door, part open to let out the heat. He kept the barrels between him and Noa the whole time, as he slipped across the threshold.

———————•⚷•———————

'We don't even know where we are,' Noa said despondently. 'Or when.' Lots of Dad's stories had been about travellers and explorers. Had he ever told her a story about this place?

The hustle and bustle all around them was so loud Noa could hardly hear herself think. Her eyes

A strategy is a plan to achieve something.

roved around the scene, taking it all in. This was a busy port, that was clear. She could hear accents and languages from all over the world. Dozens of ships were being unloaded at once and she wondered where they had travelled from. Most of the people wore dull-coloured workwear in browns and navy blue, but every now and again she saw the flash of vibrant silks or the black of a morning suit or the ridiculous height of a top hat.

She thought back to the museum's fashion display. 'I think this is the 19th century,' Noa told Renwick. 'The Victorian era.'

Renwick hopped unhappily from foot to foot. She knew he was as anxious as she was to find Grimes and the key and get home safely.

'Should we walk along the dock to search for Grimes?' Noa asked. She looked back at the cobbled courtyard and the iron door that was the way home. 'Or perhaps we should wait here until he comes back? But that could be hours, or even days.' She wasn't sure what to do for the best. Then, something occurred to her. 'Wait! We can do both. We can split up! We'll watch in shifts. He'll have to come back eventually and one of us will be here to defend the door. And the other one can explore and see if we can spy him at the docks.'

Renwick bowed his head. She knew he understood what she wanted him to do. 'You take first watch,' she said. 'If you see Grimes, fly up and call out.'

Renwick flew from her shoulder and landed on a window ledge above the iron door. Noa followed the path along the water's edge.

———————•⚷•———————

'Can you do it?' Grimes asked the locksmith. He had to raise his voice over the clamour of hammers and the hiss of hot metal that surged around them. 'Can you make a copy?'

'I can make anything you pay me to make,' the surly man said with a grunt. He was the size of a bear, with muscled arms and dark hair swept off his face.

'I want a *bad* copy,' Grimes said. 'One that looks the same but won't turn in the lock.' If Grimes

---

To defend someone or something is to protect them from an attack.

had a *fake* key, a *decoy* key, and it fell into Noa's hands, then she would think *he* was the one stuck in the Victorian era.

She wouldn't be able to resist exploring the past—she was as nosy as her parents, he was sure—and, while she was away with the fake key, he would have sufficient time to slip through the door with the real one, plus whatever treasure he could find to take home with him. Little did she realize, she would be left trapped here forever.

The locksmith raised an eyebrow. 'It'll cost you.'

Grimes smirked and held the key to the Time Door close to his chest. 'If you make a copy, I can offer you this wondrous rare coin from far-off lands.' From his pocket, he pulled a regular coin.

The locksmith looked at Grimes, then took the coin and examined it quizzically. 'Are you sure you want me to make a key that *doesn't* work?'

'That's right,' Grimes said. 'Can you do it?'

The smith wiped his hands on the front of his leather apron, leaving dark smears. 'I can do it.'

'Can you do it today?'

Sufficient means enough.

The smith glanced at his workbench, which was covered in heavy tools and bright metal parts that were waiting to be assembled. 'That will be tricky. Brunel has his fancy visitors coming later. He wants everything ship-shape for the occasion.'

Grimes reached into his pocket and brought out a second coin. 'I'll make it worth your while.'

The smith grinned. 'Come back when the noon bells chime. Your key will be ready.'

Grimes gave a smart bow to the smith and left the workshop. The noon bells couldn't be too far away. The sky outside was hazy with smoke, but it felt warm. 'It's late morning,' Grimes said to himself, smiling. 'A perfect time to find a pleasant inn for something to eat. Then I'll find Mr Brunel and see if I can get hold of a memento to take home.'

Grimes felt that luck was finally shining on him. He strolled along the street and spotted an inn on the waterfront. He could no doubt buy a fine meal of pie and mash, or jellied eels in there. Once his belly was full, then he would find Brunel's office and begin to make his fortune.

Chapter 5

Noa passed the open doors of warehouses, their insides piled high with wooden crates and bulging sacks. She passed work-sheds that radiated heat, that clanged and banged with the sound of hammers on metal. She passed inns whose doors thumped open, releasing the sound of laughter and the spicy scent of cooking.

There was no sign of Grimes anywhere.

'Penny daily! Get your news! Penny daily!' yelled a boy standing outside the nearest inn.

He waved a folded roll of newsprint in his hand. There were more newspapers in a wooden box at his feet. 'Get your news! Royal visit as SS Great Britain prepares for maiden voyage!'

Noa stopped. She tried to spy the date at the top of the page, but the boy moved it too quickly.

He smiled at her cheekily, 'If you want the news, miss, you'll have to pay for it.'

'I just wondered what the date was,' she said.

'Nothing's free in this world, miss,' he said. Then

he waved the paper and bellowed loudly, 'Penny daily! Will the iron ship sink or float?'

She was forced to step back. Noa continued along the busy walkway. So many people were focused on their work: fetching, carrying, bustling to and fro. None of them was Grimes. With every passing moment, recovering the stolen key was getting more and more unlikely.

Noa felt her eyes sting with tears.

It was at this moment that a small, scrawny-looking boy rushed through the crowd. He wasn't looking where he was going and, with a thump, he crashed right into Noa. They both went flying and Noa landed on the hard cobblestones.

'Watch where you're going, will you?' the boy shouted as he picked himself up and dusted straw from the back of his trousers.

'Me? It was you who ran through here like your shoes were on fire,' Noa snapped. But the boy wasn't listening. He was looking at the ground. He had dropped a piece of paper when he and Noa collided, and it had landed in a muddy puddle.

'Oh no!' the boy said. He hung his head. Noa could see the tidemark of dirt on his neck. His clothes looked shabby, his hair uncombed. He bent down and lifted the paper from the street. He gave it a little shake, as though that would be enough to clean off the mud.

Noa had a tissue in her pocket. 'Let me,' she said and gently took the paper. She cleaned the worst of the mess off. 'It's OK,' she said. 'You can still read what it says.'

The boy made a derisive snorting sound.

'What?' Noa asked.

'You might be able to read it. Some of us had to work instead of getting schooling.'

Noa glanced at the paper in her hand. 'Great Western Steamship Company,' she said, reading the elaborate handwriting at the top of the sheet.

The boy puffed out his chest and looked very proud of himself. 'That's right. I work for Mr Brunel now. Well, I'll work on his ship, at least. I just put my X on that contract.'

Noa's eyes travelled down the paper. She saw

the date: 19th July 1843. She was right, this was the 19th century! Then, she saw the job title written below.

'Coal hand? What's that?' she asked.

The boy grinned, and Noa could see that he truly was excited by whatever this job was. 'That's me! I'm going to be shovelling coal to make the steam to power the ship. Without me, the ship won't go anywhere. I'll get to work and travel and see the world, *and* I'll be paid six pounds a year!'

'Ten pounds a year,' Noa corrected.

'What?' The boy crumpled with confusion, his head tilted to one side, reminding Noa of Renwick.

Noa pointed to the contract. 'It says here you'll be paid ten pounds a year. I promise, that says ten pounds, not six.'

'Are you sure?' he asked.

'I'm certain. Whoever told you you'd get six pounds was wrong.'

The boy's face was shocked. 'It was the recruitment officer. Why would he say it was six pounds if the paper said ten?'

Noa felt bad for the boy. 'Did the officer know you couldn't read?'

The boy frowned. 'None of us dock hands can read. We start working as soon as we can lift a sack of oats. Everyone knows that. The officer must be keeping the extra money for himself.' The boy took the contract from Noa's hands and stared at it. 'I'm going straight back to the recruitment office. Will you come with me? In case he lies about what it says?'

She was supposed to be looking for Grimes, but this boy needed her help. 'I'll come,' she said.

The boy gave her a broad grin and set off at pace. He dived into the crowd. 'C'mon!' he shouted. Noa ran after him. She rushed past ladies in enormous skirts walking arm-in-arm; past huddles of men in dark suits who lined the pavements; past children in sailor suits and pinafores waving little flags.

'Wait!' she yelled. 'I don't even know your name!'

'It's Philip,' the boy called over his shoulder. 'Philip Glendower!'

'I'm Noa,' she said. 'Noa Goodwin.'

'Nice to meet you, Noa. Hey, Bert!' Philip waved frantically at a boy who was loading crates onto a cart. 'Bert, follow me! It will be worth your while!'

Bert scratched his head, then shouted something to the cart's driver and broke into a trot.

'Billy! Annie! Raj!' Philip yelled. More children joined the small group who followed him like the Pied Piper. There was a carnival mood as their footsteps rang out on the cobbles. With whoops and shouts, the gang of children took their collective protest to the Steamship Office.

Two storeys high with intricately carved stonework around the windows, Noa saw that it was a grander building than the warehouses and workshops.

'That's Mr Brunel's boardroom,' Philip said, pointing to a large, south-facing window on the ground floor; it had been thrown open to let in a breeze off the water. 'The recruitment office is round the back. This way.'

Philip barged straight in through the wooden door, with the dock children and Noa right behind.

A collective action or decision is done or shared by the members of a group.

He slammed the contract down on the desk in front of a pale-faced, pinched-looking young man.

'That says ten pounds a year!' Philip said.

'There's not sufficient room in here for all you urchins,' the recruitment officer said.

'We're not going anywhere,' Bert called.

'Not until you tell the truth!' Philip added. 'You told us that we'd be getting six pounds, but here, in black and white, it says ten. What happened to the other four pounds, Mr Longshanks?'

'I don't know what you're talking about.' Longshanks stood abruptly, knocking a pile of papers on his desk.

'Yes, you do!' Philip was a foot shorter than the officer, but he didn't seem at all scared. Noa was impressed. 'You're trying to take what isn't yours.'

'What on earth is going on out there?' The booming voice came from an office behind Longshanks' desk. A man stepped into the doorway and, straight away, his name was whispered among the children. Noa caught it in snatches, 'Mr Brunel', 'Isambard', 'Mr Isambard

Kingdom Brunel'. Over the chatter, Philip explained why they were there.

'Is this boy telling the truth?' Brunel demanded of Longshanks.

Longshanks blushed and muttered something that no one could make out.

'You planned on keeping back money from these children and their families?' Brunel pulled himself up to his full height and looked red with anger. 'Money that they would have rightfully earned working for my company?'

'He was planning that, sir,' Philip said quickly.

'Alfred Longshanks, you're fired,' Brunel said. 'Get out and never come back again.' Brunel started gathering the papers on Alfred's desk, moving them out of the young man's reach.

Alfred grabbed his hat and overcoat from a hatstand. He didn't even pause to put them on as he pushed past the children. A few of the taller boys snarled at him as he scurried out. But most of the children were grinning as though it were their birthdays. 'Ten pounds a year!' one girl said right in

Noa's ear. 'Such riches! I can't wait to tell Mam.'

One of the boys—Raj, was it?—clapped his hand heavily on her shoulder. 'Was it you that read the contracts? We've got to buy you a pint of Auntie Chowdary's Apple Juice to celebrate!'

The girl with dark curls, Noa thought her name was Annie, tutted in disgust. 'If it's a celebration then you're going to want Ma Wrangle's Jellied Eel Pie with mash and mint sauce. Yum!'

'I wish I could stay,' Noa said, 'but there's something I have to do. Someone I need to find.'

Noa was pleased she'd been able to help, but there was no sign of Grimes in the Steamship Offices. She hadn't spotted him on the run through the docks. If she didn't find him soon, then she should go swap places with Renwick. He might have better luck looking from the sky.

'Well,' Annie said. 'You find your friend then come and find us, you hear?' Annie and Raj waved goodbye to Noa, then headed back out to the crowded quayside. The bell above the door tinkled merrily as they left, along with the other children.

Noa was about to say her goodbyes to Philip, when she noticed the way he was staring at Brunel. He looked the way that Aunt Ada looked when she was talking about her favourite movie stars.

Philip's eyes were wide, his face awe-struck.

'Mr Brunel, sir,' Philip said tentatively.

'Yes?' Brunel smiled at Philip.

'I just wanted to say … that one day, I hope I might be a bit like you. I … I hope I might make things and be an engineer and build things that help people.'

Brunel nodded slowly. 'Well, I see no reason why, with the right opportunities and hard work, you shouldn't make your way in the world, young man.'

Philip blushed pink to the tips of his ears.

Just then, Noa heard a commotion. Beyond the heavy brown door, there were confused shouts. Then, a man with red hair burst into the front office. 'Mr Brunel! Sir, your notebook. Your personal notebook with all the details for his majesty's visit …'

'What about it?'

'It's gone, sir. Your notebook is gone.'

Chapter 6

Grimes' morning had been very pleasant indeed. He had left the locksmith, busy making the decoy key, and found an inn near the dockside. There he had persuaded the innkeeper that a handful of coins was <u>sufficient</u> payment for a lavish meal of roast chicken in gravy. With his stomach full and the Steamship Office sure to be a treasure-trove of valuable objects, he had set out to make his fortune.

It had only taken a few moments for him to learn where to find Brunel. A passing delivery boy had pointed him in the right direction. Brunel's boardroom was on the ground floor; his desk was beneath the window, where he could watch the comings-and-goings on the quay. Today, under the summer sun, the window had been thrown wide open, its casement lifted to let in a breeze and the salty fresh air. Grimes stood outside, leaning casually against the wall, beside the window, with a mounting feeling of excitement in his belly. Brunel's desk was *right there* just metres from where he

---

<u>Sufficient</u> means enough.

stood. The man himself was at work. Grimes could see a feather quill moving across writing paper with the company name at the letterhead, though from this angle, it was hard to see into the room.

He just had to be patient and wait for the perfect moment to reach inside.

The perfect moment came very soon. Some kind of angry kerfuffle was happening inside somewhere. It sounded like a gaggle of children were having a shouting competition. Grimes risked peeking in. All eyes were on the office door and whatever was going on beyond it. Not a single one of the office boys or desk clerks were looking his way. Then Brunel rose from his desk and went to investigate.

With the coast clear, Grimes reached in through the open window and lifted Brunel's leather-bound notebook from the desk. He turned away from the building and walked casually into the crowd as though he hadn't a care in the world.

Grimes' delighted grinning and triumphant cackling caused one or two of the Victorian ladies on the quayside to start in alarm.

Grimes made his way to the smith's workshop to check on the key's progress. Brunel's notebook was his!

At auction, it might make enough to pay for a plot of land, perhaps even a very small tropical island, and this was just the start! He practically tap-danced down the cobblestone street, leaping to avoid the horse droppings and gutter water. He could hear the clang of metalwork as he neared the workshop, and the smell of smoke and acrid tang of hot ore filled the air. In the distance, one set of church bells began tolling noon, before all the parish churches joined the peal. He was right on time for his appointment with the locksmith.

The enormous workshop doors were thrown open to let the heat out. Grimes stepped in and, now that the sun was high, immediately felt sweat prickle his forehead. He found the smith again with no difficulty. He glowered when he saw Grimes approach his bench.

'Ah, you're back for the key,' the smith said.

'At the agreed time,' Grime said. 'Is it ready?'

To make progress is to become better, or to make something better.

The smith reached down under the bench and lifted a small wooden box. The fake key lay inside.

It was perfect! Every detail was convincing, the funny dials, the squiggly decoration, everything except for the small chip on one of its teeth – a flaw that meant it would never turn in the Time Door lock. It would fool anyone; not even Bran would be able to discriminate between the two keys!

Grimes took his last coin from his pocket and handed it to the smith.

The smith flipped it over and sent it spinning before catching it deftly and slamming it onto the back of his hand. 'Heads!' he said triumphantly as he took a peek. 'Strange coin, this,' he said. 'Where did you say it came from again?'

'I didn't.' Grimes volunteered nothing else.

'It doesn't matter. The exchange will take it. They see coins from all over the world. They'll swap it for a shilling with Queen Victoria's fine features on it, I'm sure. Can you believe her husband will be here himself today? *The* Prince Albert! What a thing!'

To discriminate between things is to notice or show the differences between them.

Grimes froze. His fist closed tightly around the key. 'I'm sorry, say that again?' he asked.

The smith frowned. 'You know, the royal visit? His Majesty Prince Albert and probably quite a few lords and ladies of the court are all coming here this afternoon to see the iron ship. Didn't you know?'

Grimes gasped. He coughed. A royal visit? This was another opportunity for him. With a royal souvenir, he would make enough money to be able to buy a whole string of islands!

'Are you all right, sir?' the smith asked. 'You look a bit peaky.'

Grimes gave himself a stern shake. 'Yes, yes, my good man. I'm wonderful as it happens. Tell me, where exactly will the royal party be? And what time are they due to arrive?'

The smith shook his head. 'See now, that's the thing. The whole thing has been planned by Brunel and Prince Albert, you know. They've worked it all out between them, so only Brunel knows the details. He's obsessive about that sort of thing and keeps it all very close to his chest.'

Grimes felt the slight bulge of the notebook tucked into his jacket pocket. 'Does he?' Grimes said. 'Does he indeed?'

———•⚷•———

Brunel's face was grief-stricken and pale. He leaned against the desk which had belonged to Alfred. It seemed to be the only thing holding Brunel upright.

'My notebook?' he asked. 'But I left it on my desk only minutes ago!'

The office clerk nodded sadly. 'Yes, sir, I'm sorry, sir … I just checked and it wasn't there.'

'It must be!' Brunel insisted.

The clerk shook his head. He was as solemn as his black suit. 'No. I looked all over the desk and the floor beneath. It's gone, sir. The window was open.'

Brunel made a noise somewhere between a gasp and a moan. 'All of my plans. All of my latest ideas. All that progress … gone!'

Noa could hardly believe it. Brunel had come straight to Philip's defence and now this terrible thing had happened to him.

To make progress is to become better, or to make something better.

And she guessed exactly who was to blame –
Grimes! It was too much of a coincidence that
Brunel's notebook just happened to go missing on
the very day that Grimes arrived. It had to be him!

Brunel gasped again, and his hand flew to his
face. 'The arrangements for the royal visit. They
were in the notebook, too! I'd written down the
time the royal carriage is due to arrive. I'd written
the correct way to address a monarch. I'd even
written down his majesty's favourite cake, so we
had the right feast at the end of the tour, and the
exact timing of the fireworks. Without my notes,
it's all going to go wrong.'

'Don't worry,' Noa told Brunel. 'I'm going to find
that notebook for you.'

'You?' the clerk said with a smirk.

'Me,' Noa said, 'and Renwick.'

———— • ⚷ • ————

Renwick had been intently watching the cobbled
courtyard and the stretch of dockside beyond.
He'd been on guard ever since Noa had gone to
look for Grimes.

He'd circled above the area again and again. He'd seen many canal boats travel along the water, pulled by enormous shire horses on the path. He'd seen dozens of ducks and gulls following in their wake, looking out for food. He'd heard the far-off sounds of the city, hundreds of carts rumbling in the streets and a thousand voices on the wind. But he hadn't spotted Grimes.

And then, bold as brass, Grimes stepped around the side of a small chandlery that sold rope and winches and other bits needed by the boats. Grimes whistled tunelessly. He stood with his hands on his hips, staring at the water.

Renwick launched himself into the sky without another thought. 'Kwarrk!' he cried.

Noa could hear Renwick calling.

'I have to go!' she told Brunel and Philip. 'I'll be back as soon as I can.' She ran out of the office, back on to the dockside. Shading her eyes against the sun, she scanned the sky. There! Circling above the highest chimneys was Renwick.

'Renwick!' Noa called up loudly. He heard her immediately and, with impressive speed, he swept down to land on her shoulder.

'Kwarrk! Kwarrk!'

She could interpret his cry easily. He wanted her to follow him. 'Show me,' she said.

Renwick flew up, leading the way to the chandlery. Noa hurried after him, her legs pounding as she broke into a sprint. She dodged through the crowd, ducking past women in bonnets and men in tall hats. They were, she realized in a flash, wearing their best clothes for the royal visit. She jumped puddles. She swung herself around a gas-lamp and hurtled back towards the cobbled courtyard where they had all arrived. She was vaguely aware of Philip's voice, calling after her. But Noa's whole attention was on intercepting Grimes before he stepped through the iron door.

Then she saw him by a shop. Grimes was standing still, idly watching the ducks on the water.

Noa got her breathing under control. 'Grimes,' she said, with as much force as she could muster.

To interpret something is to explain or understand what it means.

He turned slowly. In his hand, Noa saw, was the key to the Never Door. 'Why,' Grimes said, 'Noa Goodwin, fancy seeing you here.'

'That key doesn't belong to you,' Noa said. 'And I think you have something else that doesn't belong to you either ... Mr Brunel's notebook.'

Grimes smiled and took a deep breath as though he was savouring the scent of the sea. 'This place has been kind to me, I must admit. But all good things must come to an end and it's *time* for me to go home. Give my best regards to Brunel, won't you?'

Grimes stepped away from the water's edge. Renwick launched himself at Grimes in a flurry of angry squawks. Grimes staggered back. He dropped the key. Noa heard it tinkle as it hit the stony ground. Renwick swooped down, twisted, and gripped the key in his beak.

'Oh no!' Grimes cried. 'The key! You've taken it from me!' He looked around the dock, as if looking for a police constable to come to his rescue.

Then, looking shifty as anything, he turned and ran down an alleyway beside the shop.

Renwick dropped the key into Noa's open palm. She had it back. She felt relieved but also confused. That had been quite easy in the end. Had Grimes given up too quickly? Pangs of worry crept over her. She felt the key's weight in her hand, and her happiness washed away any doubt. It was her responsibility to keep the Never Door safe, and, ever since Grimes had taken the key, she hadn't kept her promise. Now she could.

'You were brilliant, Renwick,' she told him.

'Kwarrk,' he replied, eyeing the path that led towards the cobbled courtyard and the iron door.

He wanted to go home, she realized. Noa shook her head sadly. 'Not quite yet, I'm sorry. Grimes has taken something important, and we need to return it to its rightful owner. But at least we have the key now: that means we can stick together.'

'Noa! Noa!' She heard Philip calling her name. He was running towards them, waving his hands.

'And,' Noa said to Renwick with a smile, 'I get the feeling it won't be just us two. We're going to have help with the search for Grimes this time.'

Chapter 7

Grimes could not have felt more delighted. Everything had worked perfectly. He had caught the raven's attention and drawn Noa in. He had dropped the fake key at exactly the right moment. Then he had fled the scene, making Noa believe that she was carrying the key to the Time Door.

But the *real* key was still tucked safely inside his pocket. He reached for it and felt the cold prongs of its teeth. He grinned. The pair wouldn't be defending the time tunnel now that they believed they had the key. As soon as he was ready, he could stroll through without a hitch.

Noa would find out eventually that the key she had was a fake, but, if she was anything like her father, thinking that objects should stay in their own time, then she wouldn't even try to use it until she had recovered Brunel's notebook. All he had to do was lie low and wait for the coast to be clear.

Grimes walked the alleyway, avoiding the rank-smelling drain that ran down its centre. He

To defend someone or something is to protect them from an attack.

was heading for the cobbled courtyard.

He should go straight home.

That was the sensible thing to do.

The alley opened up beside the warehouses. Suddenly, he was among the crowd, all dressed in their finery. Bonnets and bouquets, ribbons and ringlets: everyone wearing their best for Prince Albert.

His hand went to his pocket where Brunel's notebook rested. Inside were all the complex details of the royal visit. It was a chance too good to miss. What harm would one small detour do?

There was nothing Grimes hated more than letting an opportunity slip through his fingers.

———— •🗝• ————

Philip had caught up with Noa outside the chandlery. He was speaking quickly. 'All of the children you helped want to say thank you properly,' Philip was saying. 'Without you, Mr Longshanks would have been able to keep all the money that was owed to us. Annie and Raj want to throw a party in your honour. Say you'll come.'

Complex means complicated or difficult, because of having a lot of different parts.

Noa looked towards the alleyway where Grimes had disappeared. She had the key back now, but before she could go home, she had to do all that she could to reunite Brunel with his notebook. If she hadn't let Grimes take the key in the first place, then none of this would have happened. It was partly her fault the notebook was gone.

'Hello? Noa? You're not listening!' Philip said.

'Kwarrk!' Renwick cawed.

'Even your raven thinks so,' Philip said, eyeing the bird warily.

'He's called Renwick.'

The flow of people, all heading in the same direction, was increasing. It was getting hard to see. The tall hats and high bonnets that the grown-ups wore made her feel very short.

'There's a party in your honour – will you come?' Philip said again.

'I have to find a man called Grimes. I can't tell you how I know, but he's the person who took Brunel's notebook. I last saw him here a few minutes ago. He can't have gone far.'

Philip looked serious. Noa knew he'd want to help Brunel just as much as she did. 'All right, how about this? We get all the children together and you tell them exactly who they're looking for. We all search the docks until we find him and the notebook. Then the party can be a double celebration – a triple celebration if you count the royal visit!'

'That would be wonderful!' Noa said. A collective effort to search was much more likely to find Grimes than working alone.

'Right,' Philip said. 'We're to meet Annie at Ma Wrangle's Pie Shop. Let's go!'

Ma Wrangle's Pie Shop was set back from the canal, down a narrow lane. On either side, wharf buildings blocked out the sky and it seemed as though the delicious smells of warm pastry and gravy were being channelled right towards them. Noa's belly rumbled – it had been a while since the cheese on toast at supper.

Philip pushed open a dark, crooked door and the sound of laughter and thin wisps of steam

A collective action or decision is done or shared by the members of a group.

escaped from inside. Noa and Renwick followed him in. The shop was small, Noa realized, not much bigger than the sitting room at home. But every wall, every surface was crammed with objects: the wooden tables were set with earthenware pots of salts and sauces, and plates piled high with golden pies; the walls were decorated with framed cross-stitch pictures and drawings, and on the ceiling rows and rows of jugs hung, next to cups on hooks. There was something to look at everywhere. Around the objects were people, most of them children she recognized from the recruitment office. There were Raj, Bert and Billy – she gave them a wave. And there was Annie, talking to a smiling woman with a white apron who must have been Ma Wrangle.

'Noa!' Annie cried when she spotted her. 'And who's this?' she asked gazing in wonder at Renwick.

'This is Renwick. He's my friend,' Noa said. 'Renwick, this is Annie.'

Renwick cawed a greeting and Annie laughed, her dark curls bobbing around her face. 'Well, you

are a wonder and a half.' She turned to the room, looking excited. 'Everyone, our guest of honour is here.' There were whoops and cheers from the children assembled. Noa felt herself blush, but Annie was grinning right at her, so she let herself smile back.

'Thanks to Noa,' Philip said to the assembly, 'we are all going to have more money to send back home.' There were more cheers at that. 'But right now, Noa needs our help. She's chasing a man who, we have reason to believe, has taken Brunel's notebook.' The cheers turned to boos.

'What can we do?' Annie asked.

'Help me find him,' Noa said. 'He's tall, with blonde hair and pale skin. He's wearing a suit, but no hat, and the cut of his jacket might look very unfashionable to you. As soon as we have the notebook back, then we can celebrate properly.'

'Here, take this for now.' Philip handed Noa a pie. It was still warm and smelled of butter and spices. She took it gratefully and ate it in three big bites. She fed the crust to Renwick, who was just as pleased.

'Here's the strategy,' Annie told the children. 'We're going to spread out around the docks. If any of you spot him, get word back to me.' She turned to Noa, 'I've got a good job now with the Steamship, but time was when I was the best sharp between here and St Paul's.'

'What's a sharp?' Noa asked.

'Let's just say that if we want to get that notebook back, without your Mr Grimes noticing that anything at all is amiss, then what you want is a sharp,' Annie said with a wink.

Philip wiped pie crumbs from his chest. 'Annie used to do card tricks, sleight-of-hand magic, that sort of thing,' he explained. 'She'd throw down a cap and perform for passers-by. She can make an egg come out of your ear, if you ask her nicely.'

'I'd make people's pocket-watches pop out of their nostril. That was my favourite trick,' Annie said. 'The old skills will come in handy on this job. Right, let's find your Mr Grimes.'

Noa realized that the shop was empty and most of the plates were clean. All the children—dozens

A **strategy** is a plan to achieve something.

of them—had flooded out into the street to search. She felt her heart lift; with this much help, she would be on her way back to Aunt Ada and the museum in no time.

———————•⚷•———————

Noa and Renwick, Philip and Annie left the shop, heading back up to the path beside the water. From there, they joined the flow of people heading towards the dock. Somewhere nearby Noa heard a church bell peal the time, once, twice.

'All these people must be going to the iron ship, the SS Great Britain, to see the prince,' Noa whispered to Renwick.

She edged past a family with half a dozen children, the oldest of whom had stopped in the centre of the road to collect a fallen baby's rattle. She was careful to keep Philip and Annie in sight. 'I hope we can get the notebook back before Brunel has to meet the prince. He was so worried about it.'

'Kwarrk,' Renwick said reassuringly.

She wanted to stay positive, but the crowd

was getting so big it was getting harder to walk, let alone find Grimes. This was going to be an <u>intensive</u> search.

Then, she noticed that Philip and Annie were waving to her. They were standing next to a crane. It was, Noa guessed, for loading and unloading the boats as they moved through the dock. It reminded her of a mini Eiffel Tower. Its metal frame rose up towards the sky and an arm arched out over the water. On one side, the crane's metal struts formed a ladder. Annie was already climbing up to get a clearer view of the crowd. It was wide enough that Philip and Noa were able to climb alongside her.

Once they were above the heads of the crowd, they scanned the area. The sky above was a warm blue, with wisps of cloud over in the direction of the city. Gulls whirled and searched for their next snack. Below, the heads of the people bobbed like waves on the sea.

Noa realized it was easier to look for a head without a hat. It was only the children who were

Intensive activity involves a lot of effort over a short time.

hatless – the children and Grimes. This should discriminate him from others in the crowd. Her eyes swept from side to side. Renwick circled too.

'Is that him?' Annie pointed.

Grimes' blonde hair stood out like a sore thumb. 'That's Grimes!' Noa cheered.

'Gotcha!' Annie said. She shimmied down the ladder. 'I'll be right back.'

———————•⚷•———————

Grimes was certain he had made the right decision. Yes, he had Brunel's notebook, and that was good. But to have a memento from Prince Albert himself? Well, that would be excellent. He owed it to himself to make the most of the opportunity. As long as he was careful and didn't run into Noa again, he would be absolutely fine, he was sure. So, he'd followed his nose, and the crowd, towards the dock right at the end of the quayside, where the SS Great Britain was waiting to be launched. He paused to watch a juggler who had set up a cap and was performing for the street urchins. It was all very entertaining.

To discriminate between things is to notice or show the differences between them.

Then, a rather dirty-looking girl, with dark curls and a cheeky air about her, ran right into him. They both tumbled to the ground with a thump.

The girl sprang to her feet. 'Oh, I am so sorry, sir,' she said. 'I didn't see you there. Are you hurt?' She grabbed his hand and pulled him up.

He stood slowly, winded.

The key! Did he still have the key?

He reached into his pocket and felt its comforting weight.

The girl was beating the dust from his jacket front. 'Oh dear, such a mess. I am so sorry, sir.'

He glared at her. 'You should take more care,' he snapped impatiently.

'Yes, sir, I will,' she said, already heading into the crush of people. In a second, she was out of sight.

Grimes, still gripping the key, carried on through the crowd.

Chapter 8

Annie danced back towards the spot where Noa, Renwick and Philip waited. Noa could tell, the moment she saw Annie, that her mission had been successful. She was grinning from ear to ear.

'You got the notebook back?' Noa asked.

'I did!' Annie held out Brunel's notebook. 'Grimes didn't notice a thing!'

Annie's actions had got the notebook back for its rightful owner. Noa was pleased that it had been done without causing a scene. 'Thank you,' she said. Noa took the notebook from Annie and handed it to Philip. 'Here, you give it back to Brunel.'

'Me?' Philip raised his palm to his chest.

'Yes. He's your hero. You should get the chance to speak to him again – maybe you could ask him if he's looking for a new apprentice?'

'Don't you want to deliver it?' Philip asked.

Noa shook her head. It was time to go home. This visit had been interesting, and eventful. She'd met some lovely new friends, eaten a delicious pie, and helped to put things right. But she wasn't supposed to be here. She had been lucky – nothing had gone so terribly wrong that she hadn't been able to put it right. Now, though, she should go back to her own time.

'I have to go,' she told Philip and Annie. 'Thank you for everything.'

She gave them both a hug. Philip looked sad to see her go and even Annie's smile dimmed a little. Renwick cawed a goodbye too.

Philip and Annie headed towards the SS Great Britain: that would be the right place to find Brunel and return his notebook. Noa headed in the other direction. She had to walk against the flow of the crowd which made it very slow going.

Renwick flew up to scan for shortcuts. 'Kwarrk!' He swooped down and headed into an alley. Noa followed. Like the alleyway where she'd found Ma Wrangles' Pie Shop, this was dark, overshadowed by damp brickwork. The gloom settled on her.

'Renwick,' she said. 'Do you think that it's right for us to leave Grimes here?'

Renwick settled back on her shoulder. She wished he could answer, but though he couldn't speak, he was still a very good listener, and she felt she could interpret his thoughts.

'If we leave and take the key with us, then Grimes is going to be stuck in 1843. He'll grow old here, with no way to get home.' Noa kicked a stone that skittered into a gutter.

Renwick cawed sympathetically.

They reached the end of the alleyway. She followed the building around past narrow windows and closed doors and turned into the cobbled courtyard. The warehouse with the iron door was right in front of them.

She didn't trust Grimes one little bit. But did that mean it was right to leave him behind? 'Dad would know what to do,' she told Renwick.

That was it! She knew that Dad would be home one day. He had to be. And when he came home, she would tell him about Grimes, and Dad could travel back to 1843 to rescue him! Grimes wouldn't be here long, not even if she didn't tell Dad for

To interpret something is to explain or understand what it means.

weeks and weeks … that was the brilliance of time travel!

With a lighter heart, Noa approached the iron door. She glanced around, to be sure that no-one was watching, but there were hardly any people here now – they had all gone to watch the royal arrival. It was just her and Renwick. Noa took out the key and slipped it into the lock.

'Ready?' she asked Renwick.

'Kwarrk.'

Noa turned the key.

Nothing happened.

Noa tried again, but the key just wouldn't turn in the lock. She felt her pulse quicken. A horrible cold shiver ran through her. Why wouldn't the door open? This was the right one, wasn't it? Her head whipped left and right as she scanned the side of the warehouse. Yes, this was definitely the right door. All the others were wooden. She rattled the key in the lock. It made no difference. 'It won't open,' Noa said. 'The Never Door won't open!'

Grimes pushed through the crowd, with his nose wrinkled in disgust. The crush of people smelled of over-boiled vegetables and sweat. *Perhaps this wasn't such a good idea after all?* he thought.

'Oi!' a woman carrying a crying baby complained as he elbowed his way forward. Grimes didn't apologize; he was finally through to the front.

He looked up, and gasped.

A few police constables were keeping an open space clear between the buildings of the dockside and the SS Great Britain. Which meant that, for the very first time, Grimes could see the steamship.

It was enormous. Huge. Mammoth. Its iron hull, which had been painted in crisp lines of red, black and white, towered above him like an elephant next to a mouse. It was long too, much longer than he had been expecting. From the tip of its prow to its stern it must have been 100 metres long. Above the deck, bristling up into the blue sky were its masts. There were no sails unfurled as yet; instead flags the size of bed sheets fluttered from them in celebration. It was a wonder. Any single object that he took from the ship back to his own time would fetch an excellent price at auction.

A gangway led down from the ship to the quay. Officials gathered at the bottom of the gangway – some in black suits, others looking more like sailors. The handrail was adorned with ribbons and flowers. Then Grimes spotted a carriage pulled by four horses coming round the corner. The carriage gleamed to a high polish. The horses raised their feet neatly as though dancing.

Prince Albert had arrived.

Noa looked at the key on her palm, the key that wouldn't turn in the lock. Now that she examined it closely, she could see that this wasn't her key. It was very similar, but one of the teeth was chipped. It didn't have the elegant craftsmanship of the real key. This one had been made in a hurry.

'This isn't my key,' she exclaimed, her hands shaking.

Renwick fluttered his wings in alarm.

'Grimes must have had this made and dropped it deliberately so that we'd stop guarding the door.' Noa felt as if the ground was swaying underneath her feet. 'Without the key, we can't get home. We're stuck in 1843!' A worse thought occurred to her. 'What if Grimes has already gone back through? What if he's already left 1843 with the real key?' If that were true, then she might never see home again. Dad wouldn't know where to look for her. Aunt Ada would come home to an empty museum and not have the first idea of where she had gone. It was unbearable.

Noa pressed her palms against the iron door. She knew it wouldn't open without the Never Door key, but it was good to lean against its cool metal and gather her thoughts. She took a few slow breaths. When she felt a little stronger, she stood up.

'This isn't over yet,' she told Renwick. 'There's a chance that Grimes is still here in 1843. Especially if he noticed that he doesn't have Brunel's notebook any more. Grimes is greedy. We have to hope that greed has made him stay. And, if he is still here, then we still have a chance to find the real key. We need Philip's help. We have to get to the SS Great Britain,' Noa said.

———— •⚷• ————

Grimes could feel the electric excitement of the crowd as the carriage rolled up. There must have been hundreds of people lining this one path. Gentlemen and ladies waved handkerchiefs enthusiastically; labourers and workers of all kinds had paused their tasks in the hope of catching sight of the royal visitor; children weaved between the legs of the adults, vying for a better spot. Grimes was right at the front. He had an excellent view as the carriage pulled up smartly at the bottom of the gangway. There was Brunel, easy to pick out in his tall top hat, waiting to open the carriage door and welcome the prince. Grimes wondered at the appearance of two children who stood beside Brunel. Neither looked to have been tidied up in preparation for meeting Prince Albert. One was a pale-looking boy, the other a girl with a knotted tangle of dark curls who looked strangely familiar. Where had Grimes seen that girl before? He couldn't quite place her.

Then, just as Brunel was about to step forward and make the first greeting, Grimes noticed something very odd. Very odd indeed. Brunel seemed to be checking something in a book that looked exactly like the notebook that Grimes had taken from Brunel's desk. Grimes' mouth dropped open. He checked his pockets. He re-checked his pockets. The notebook wasn't there. How was that possible? How on earth had the notebook gone from Grimes' pocket to Brunel's hand? It didn't make any sense. Grimes staggered a little.

'Hey, watch where you're stepping,' the lean

young man beside Grimes snarled.

'What? Oh, yes,' Grimes replied, still reeling at his discovery. He had no idea how he had lost the notebook or how that same notebook had found its way back to Brunel, but he had a fair guess who might be responsible – Noa Goodwin.

———— •✎• ————

Noa and Renwick heard the nearby church bells chime three. The sun was high in the sky and the narrow alleyways seemed to sweat in the heat. She had stuck to the alleyways to avoid the crowd, which meant, when she finally arrived at the dock, she found herself bursting out into the warm sunshine and the colossal sight of the iron ship.

'Wow!' she said.

She had seen big ships before, but there was something magical about the SS Great Britain. To see a ship that was big enough to cross oceans, that had no fewer than six giant masts all bedecked with billowing flags, took her breath away. No wonder all the children were excited to be part of its crew.

The crowd between Noa and the ship was dwarfed by the huge iron hull. It was as though a mountain were about to set sail.

'How will we find anyone in this crowd?' Noa worried. If only she could fly like Renwick, she could have swooped over the crowd. As it was, she had to nudge and elbow her way through. She was sure that Annie and Philip would be as close to the action as possible; right at the front, she suspected. She eased her way past ladies with parasols and men in fine suits. 'Sorry, excuse me, sorry, thank you.'

Finally, she made it through the crowd and could see the gangway and the royal carriage properly for the first time. There was Brunel!

And, standing next to Brunel, about to meet the prince, were Philip and Annie!

Noa felt a surge of joy for them, despite her worry. Her friends must have made Brunel very happy indeed when they returned his lost notebook. 'Right,' Noa said to Renwick. 'Let's go and ask for their help.'

Grimes clenched his jaw and balled his fists. He had no idea how Noa Goodwin had done it, but somehow Brunel had his notebook back. Grimes had absolutely nothing to show from his time in 1843.

But, he realized, it wasn't over yet. There was still the chance to scoop an even bigger prize. Right at this very second, Brunel reached out and opened the door to the royal carriage. A footman scooted close and pulled down the step. Prince Albert stepped out. The crowd erupted into celebration, cheering and clapping.

Prince Albert was a tall man with a moustache. He wore a navy jacket with gleaming gold buttons and a polished medal on his chest. He looked enormously interested in the iron ship before him. Grimes remembered that the Prince had a reputation for being obsessed with inventions of all kinds.

Prince Albert. Husband of Queen Victoria. The actual Prince Albert! Grimes felt his spirits rise.

To be obsessed with something, or to obsess over something, is to be continually thinking about it.

The prince waved and smiled at the crowd. Grimes may have lost the notebook, but something much better had come along. This was an opportunity he wouldn't miss.

Grimes watched as the two children with Brunel were introduced to the prince. Then some of the engineers in suits and the sailors in uniforms gave smart salutes as he moved by. Prince Albert was to be given a guided tour, first along the outside of the ship to admire its hull. Later, Grimes remembered from the notebook, he would be taken on board where tea and cake would be waiting.

Prince Albert, he noticed, walked with a cane. It was elegant and slender, made of a dark wood and tipped with silver at either end. It was just the sort of thing that might take pride of place in a museum, or sell for a lot of money at an auction …

Grimes grinned. Now he just needed to find a strategy to acquire the cane without the prince, the crew, or the crowd of two hundred people noticing. What he needed was a diversion.

———————— •⚷• ————————

A strategy is a plan to achieve something.

Noa had eased her way under elbows, over bags and around bodies to reach the front of the crowd.

'Annie! Philip!' she called.

Philip heard her call. He raced over, with Annie right behind. 'You came back!' he said, in delight. 'Just in time too. Brunel was so pleased to get his notebook back, he let us meet the prince. Look, they're over there!'

He pointed to where the prince greeted the smiling faces of the people who lined the quay. Brunel hovered behind him, helping to gather the small posies of flowers that some of the children in the crowd offered.

Noa forced a smile. She tried her best to look pleased that the day had turned out so well for her friends. But she can't have done a very good job of it.

'What is it?' Annie asked. 'What's the matter?'

Noa felt tears prickle her eyes at the question. 'Oh,' she said. 'I'm sorry, I don't want to be a bother.'

Annie put her arm around Noa's shoulder. 'Come over here.' Annie led Noa away from the carriage

and the crowd. The SS Great Britain was so huge that its hull curved up out of the dock and created a kind of shelter underneath. It was to this quieter spot that Annie guided Noa. Philip found a couple of sandbags that were ready to be used against the swell of water when the ship was launched.

He arranged them quickly, so that they had somewhere more comfortable to sit than the ground. In the shadow of the hull, Noa felt a little bit better. She could hear the distant cheering of the crowd and some kind of brass band was playing a cheerful tune. The waves lapped gently at the side of the ship below the dock.

'Tell us, what happened?' Philip asked.

With Renwick cawing encouragingly, Noa told them as much as she could without revealing the secret of the Never Door. 'Grimes tricked me,' she said. 'He has the key to my house. It's the only one, and, unless I get it back, I can't go home,' she said.

'Aren't your mother and father at home? Can't they let you in?' Philip asked.

Noa shook her head. 'I live with my aunt.

I haven't seen my mother or father for a really, really long time,' she said, perfectly truthfully. 'I can't really explain, but I can't get to my aunt without the key, and Grimes has it.'

'I'm sorry,' Annie said. 'But we found him once – we can find him again!'

'Yes,' said Philip. 'We won't let him get away with it. He can't keep you from your family.' Philip's eyes rested for a moment on the black paintwork of the ship above them. 'It doesn't matter how far away from home you travel. If you care about your family and they care about you, then nothing should keep you from getting home safe and sound to them. Nothing.'

Noa realized that Philip was thinking of his voyage to come: crossing the Atlantic on a ship that was brand new, that had an iron hull where every ship that had ever gone before it was made of wood. He was thinking of his own family that he would leave behind.

'You're right,' Noa said. 'Grimes isn't going to stop me from getting home. But he could be anywhere.

He might not even still be at the harbour.'

It was at that moment that the cacophony started.

Grimes needed a distraction. Something that would divert the attention of the crowd and all the crew and officials, while he helped himself to Prince Albert's silver-tipped cane. But what?

The crowd were making enough noise already, cheering the prince. A brass band had just started playing; the cornet and trombone blasted rousing songs that some of the onlookers joined in with. The prince had almost reached the end of the ship and would soon be headed up the gangway and on board … and once that happened, the chance would be gone.

Just then, Grimes spotted the perfect solution to his problem. At the end of the dock, out past the crowd was a wooden platform, like a school stage. On top of that platform was an array of cardboard tubes on wooden canes.

They looked like little toy rockets. A small boy, sitting cross-legged and looking very fed up, guarded the scene. Grimes recalled the instructions in Brunel's notebook – when the ship was finally launched, it would do so to a barrage of fireworks. It seemed a pity to have fireworks in the daytime, but the Victorians were famous for their love of display.

Grimes sidled up to the boy. 'Hello,' he said. 'Seems you were the unlucky one today?'

The boy looked up, startled. 'What was that, sir?'

Grimes plastered on his most sincere smile. 'I was observing, it's unfortunate that you were given the worst job. Sitting here watching it all from afar?'

The boy nodded sadly. 'Yes. My big brother Jack supplied the fireworks, but he wanted to see the prince. So, I'm stuck here until he comes back.'

Grimes eyed the wooden platform. Nailed to the rickety makeshift poles, he could spot Catherine Wheels, Squibs and Crackers and more.

Each had a short fuse hanging below and Grimes could see a small tinderbox smouldering in readiness, though it wasn't needed for an hour or so.

'It seems such a shame for you to miss out,' he

said. 'Tell you what. I've just come from the ship. I've seen the prince already. How about I mind the display for you for five minutes? You can run and see the prince, then run back here and Jack won't even know you were gone.'

The boy's eyes brightened. 'Oh, would you, sir?'

'I would, young man.'

He leapt up, his face gleaming with delight. 'I won't be long, sir.' His smile faded. 'You won't go touching nothing, will you, sir? Jack has set up the most complex display we've done yet. He'd be awful cross to find anything changed.'

Grimes gave another tight smile. 'I promise I won't.'

With that reassurance, the boy moved away at a skip. He seemed thrilled to be allowed to leave his post. Grimes reached for the tinderbox.

———————•🗝•———————

Noa, Philip and Annie leapt up from the sandbags at the first sound of the commotion. Bangs! Huge bangs and blasts and whizzes.

'What on earth?' Philip said. He moved out from their shelter and looked to the crowd. Right at

---

Complex means complicated or difficult, because of having a lot of different parts.

the other end of the ship, where Prince Albert had nearly finished his tour, a small wooden shelter – it looked a bit like a garden shed with the front wall missing, Noa thought – appeared to be exploding.

Whizz-CRACK!

Whizz-CRACK!

Whizz-CRACK … the shed boomed.

Noa recognized the sound and blare of fireworks. The sun was too bright to see their sparks and shimmers, but the smoke billowed out thickly in all directions.

A figure, hidden by the smoke cloud, ducked into the crowd.

Boom! Bang! Pop-pop-pop-pop!

The crowd, surprised by the sudden shrieks and howls, moved away. Some people moved too quickly. The brass band had fallen silent. Bodies pushed and pummelled each other. There was a shout and a fall.

The prince must have noticed the danger, too. He dropped his walking stick to the ground, and the flowers he was carrying, and raced to Brunel. Noa watched the prince shout something urgently in Brunel's ear. Brunel climbed on top of one of the huge barrels that were waiting to be loaded onto the ship and faced the crowd.

'Good people!' Brunel called. No one listened. He raised his arms and yelled. 'Everyone!' The trumpeter, noticing Brunel's cry, gave a short sharp blast on his trumpet. The crowd jumped.

'Good townspeople!' Brunel said into the pause. 'Don't worry. It's just the fireworks going off too soon. Quiet yourselves, there's nothing to fear.'

It was working. Apart from one small boy, who ran from the crowd and looked distraught at the smouldering stack of used fireworks, everyone

relaxed. A few people even began to laugh. Noa let out a relieved sigh. The panic ebbed away from the crowd like water down a drain.

All the fireworks were finished. Cautiously, the brass band started to play again and the crowd fell back to line the dock once more.

Noa watched as Brunel was helped down from the barrel by the sailors. Prince Albert shook his hand warmly; their action had stopped anyone in the crowd from being hurt. Another sailor collected as many of the dropped posies as he could. He turned one way, then the other, checking the ground. Noa realized that the sailor was looking for something. He looked over to the prince. The sailor's shoulders drooped, as though he had bad news to deliver.

The prince's walking stick, Noa thought – it wasn't anywhere to be seen. Someone had taken it! And she knew exactly who it must have been.

Chapter 10

'Grimes has taken the prince's walking stick!' Noa said urgently. 'Now he'll be trying to escape!' Renwick reacted immediately. He launched himself up into the air and trained his eyes on the crowd. Noa and Annie ran as fast as they could towards the firework platform, now grey and smoking.

'At least we know he's still here,' Noa muttered.

Philip didn't follow the girls. Instead, he skirted around the edge of the crowd, going the long way round to reach the back. He hoped that Grimes would find it slow going to push past everyone. If Philip was quick, he'd be able to cut Grimes off.

With her and Annie going one way, Philip the other and Renwick watching from above, Noa hoped that Grimes would be caught, by their collective effort, in a pincer movement.

———— • ⚷ • ————

Grimes hid the silver-tipped cane under his jacket as he pushed his way through the crowd. The fireworks had been better than he'd even

---

A collective action or decision is done or shared by the members of a group.

imagined. Not a single soul had seen him. Now he just had to make it to the Time Door.

'Kwarrk! Kwarrk!'

The sound of a raven calling angrily made a few of the people around him look up. A murmur ran through the crowd at the strange behaviour of the bird. Grimes cursed. He had no hat to hide his head, so instead he tried to pull his jacket collar up and kept his gaze down on the ground. But it was no good. He had been spotted.

———•⚷•———

'Kwarrk!' Renwick cried out.

'We're coming,' Noa shouted. She kept one hand gripped tightly in Annie's, so that they wouldn't get separated as they followed Grimes.

'Kwarrk!' Renwick called again.

'This way!' Noa shouted, as she swerved a family of identically dressed girls. Noa urged Annie on. 'We're getting close,' she said. She could tell they were headed the right way, not just because of Renwick's cries, but also because the crowd was thinning a little. The strange behaviour of the raven, circling

the man and calling again and again had drawn their attention. People were confused and a little bit frightened, so they moved away from Grimes.

It meant that Grimes was in a small island of empty space when Noa and Annie burst through. From the other side of the clearing came Philip, joined by Raj and Billy.

'Grimes!' Noa called. 'You're surrounded. There's nowhere to go. Return the walking stick and the key, right this minute.'

Noa realized that everyone in the crowd was looking their way: they had a hundred witnesses. Grimes had to listen. What choice did he have?

She soon had her answer. Grimes turned on his heel and shoved a lady in a green dress, carrying a matching parasol, to one side. He charged into the gap she left. He was shoving and pushing and forcing his way back towards the SS Great Britain. Noa saw one young man in a tweed suit fall to the floor; others hurried to help him up.

'After him!' Philip called.

There was no need to ask twice. Everyone was on

Grimes' tail … Philip, Noa, Annie, Raj and Billy. Then, behind them, the young man in the tweed suit and the woman waving her green parasol furiously.

Grimes had a lead, but they were catching him up.

'Stop!' Noa shouted. But there was too much commotion now for anyone to pay heed. The brass band launched into a loud *oom-pah*, *oom-pah* sound with a cymbal clashing on every other beat.

'Stop!' she cried again.

It was no use. Grimes had made it through the crowd and was scurrying up the gangway. He was headed onto the ship itself!

The engineers in suits saw what was happening. No one was supposed to board the ship before the prince! Five angry engineers raced up the gangway after Grimes.

Then Noa and the other children clattered up.

Then Brunel, curious as to why all these people were running uninvited onto his ship, followed.

Finally—wondering what could be so important, that it would interrupt such a momentous occasion and cause Brunel to leave his side—came Prince

Albert, accompanied by his guards.

Everyone chased Grimes up the gangway and onto the deck of the SS Great Britain.

Noa barely had any time to take in the view from the deck of the ship – but it was too wondrous to just ignore. The floor was made of smooth planks of wood that stretched from prow to stern in golden strips. The six enormous masts, now that she could see them up close, were thick as old oak trunks, and so tall that they seemed to reach up to the clouds.

'It's amazing!' Noa gasped.

'Why, thank you,' Brunel said.

There was Grimes, running as fast as he could, along the deck. The engineers were right behind him. He glanced back over his shoulder. She could see the panic on his face.

Where was he going? He was going to run out of ship, and then it was just the cold water below.

Noa followed the engineers. They were all shouting at Grimes to stop.

Annie, Raj, Billy and Philip called for Grimes to return the walking stick he'd taken.

Grimes pressed up against the railing that ran all the way around the ship. He gripped the edge with both hands. Seemingly still trying to push himself as far away from the gathering as possible, without falling in the water.

He had come to the end.

Noa walked slowly over to where he cowered. She moved to the front of the shouting crowd and called out to him, 'Dr Grimes!' One by one, the group fell silent, curious about the girl who knew the stranger's name. For a moment, Noa felt the warm afternoon sun on her face and smelled the tang of fireworks still clinging to the air.

'Dr Grimes,' she repeated. 'You've made all these people cross, but you can put it right if you want to. All you have to do is say sorry and give back the things that don't belong to you.'

Grimes' eyes ran over the throng, seeing one angry face after another. 'I don't have anything that doesn't belong to me,' he insisted. He wasn't going to let a child take away the thing he'd worked so hard for. He was owed this treasure.

'I think you do,' Noa said, drawing confidence from the crowd around her. 'I think you have something that belongs to the prince, and I think you have something that belongs to me. You have no right to keep them.'

'Lies!' Grimes cried dramatically. 'I'm a respectable businessman. I haven't taken anything.' He flung out his arm in protest. But, from the inside of his jacket, there fell an elegant black walking stick tipped at either end in silver.

The crowd gasped. Prince Albert stalked forward and snatched up his cane. 'This is mine!' he said. 'Guards! Fetch me an officer of the law. They must defend the Queen's peace!'

It was probably what Grimes deserved, Noa thought, to be arrested and tried. But, if he went to prison then he risked getting stuck here forever – and without the key, so did she.

The prince pulled himself up to his full height and glared at Grimes. 'The young lady was right about you. Return whatever else you took immediately.'

Grimes looked shifty; he avoided the prince's gaze.

To defend someone or something is to protect them from an attack.

'Return the young lady's possessions right this instant!' Prince Albert demanded.

Grimes, facing an angry crowd on one side and a drop down into the harbour on the other, had no choice. There wasn't sufficient time to think of another plan. Bitterly, he reached a shaking hand into his pocket. Slowly, reluctantly, he pulled out the key to the Never Door. Noa knew straight away that it was the real one this time, because she could see the inscription peeping out on its side: 'Noa – to find your way home'. That was the key that her parents had created for her. The key they'd made so that, no matter what happened, she could always get home. The thought of the museum, and Aunt Ada, and above all, Dad, put a lump in her throat.

Prince Albert took the key from Grimes and passed it to Noa. As soon as it was in her hand, she felt such a rush of emotion – relief, joy, contentment, but most of all she felt hope. Hope that now she could get home.

Noa heard the heavy tramping of boots on the

Sufficient means enough.

wooden deck. Police officers in black uniforms with funny hats marched across the ship to where the group stood. Grimes was going to be arrested!

'Wait,' Noa said. She turned to Grimes urgently. The officers paused. 'Dr Grimes,' she said. 'Please, tell everyone you're sorry and you'll never do it again.' She stepped so close to Grimes that only he could hear her as she whispered, 'If you go to prison, there will be no way back to our time. If you say sorry, they might let you go. We can go back through the iron door together, if you just say you're sorry.'

For a second, Noa thought she had convinced him. His eyes widened as he imagined life in a Victorian prison.

Then, the look was gone and there was nothing but contempt on Grimes' face. 'Me? Say sorry? It's Bran who should say sorry to me. He's the one who kept the key and Time Door secret and swindled me out of my rightful reward.' He raised his gaze to the crowd. 'I'm not sorry for anything!'

Prince Albert signalled to the police officers. It was over in a matter of moments. Grimes was

practically lifted between two of the most burly-looking officers and swept back to the gangway, quicker than Noa could blink.

Her fingers tightened on the key. Grimes had chosen his path. But, when she and Dad were finally reunited, she would tell him everything and maybe he would be able to help Grimes in the future, or in the past, or whatever it was.

'What an eventful afternoon,' Brunel said. 'And we still have the cake and the launch of the ship to go!'

Prince Albert grinned. 'Is it time for cake? Have you got any fruit cake? I'm very partial to it.'

'Yes, sir, I believe we do,' Brunel said. 'Follow me!'

Brunel led the prince and the engineers down to the lower levels of the ship.

Noa, Renwick and the children were left alone on deck. High above, she could hear gulls circling in the bright summer sunshine. Noa knew her time here was over, for now.

Philip stepped forward. 'You're not coming to eat cake, are you?' he asked Noa sadly.

She shook her head. 'I'm sorry, but it's time for

me to go,' she said.

'Will we see you again?' Annie asked.

Noa didn't know what the future held, but she thought there would be plenty of adventures in store for all of them. 'Never say never,' she said.

She gave everyone a hug in turn. Philip was last. 'Thank you,' he said as he let go. 'Without you we'd never have got our pay rise, or met Brunel, and now we're going to eat fruit cake with the prince! You changed my life.'

'Well,' Noa said. 'You deserve it. You're all wonderful.' She felt tears welling, but they were happy tears this time. 'Good luck! Goodbye, everyone. Goodbye!'

She and Renwick headed back to the gangway and down to the dock. Once they were beyond the crowd it was easy to make their way back to the iron door. This time, when Noa put the key in the lock, it turned easily.

She turned the handle. She was more than ready to go home.

Chapter 11

Noa and Renwick stepped into the time tunnel. Her heart leapt to see the swirling pink and purple lights and hear the familiar sound of wind rising.

She was lifted off her feet and was soon floating back towards the Never Door. Noa was trying to learn to enjoy the sensation of travelling, even though it was still so new to her. Gazing at Renwick gliding alongside her, Noa took a deep breath to steady her nerves and stretched out her arms as if she were flying. Side tunnels flashed past, hundreds of possibilities of time, but she was heading home.

Bam! Something—someone—shot from a side tunnel, and barrelled right into her and Renwick. They tumbled and span in the air.

She beat her arms to steady herself, just like Renwick would. As she regained control, she peered towards the figure. If the wind hadn't been holding her up, she was sure she would have dropped to the floor in shock.

The person she'd collided with looked for all the world like Dr Bran Goodwin. Like her dad.

She pushed closer to them to get a better look. The time wind fought against her. Renwick cawed his encouragement.

The person patted themselves down cautiously, as though worried they might be hurt. He looked right at her.

'Dad? Dad, is that you?'

'Noa!'

That one word brought tears to her eyes. There was so much love, and concern, and fear, and joy in it. It was her dad! He looked thinner and paler than last time she had seen him, but it was definitely Dad.

The wind still swirled, ready to pull her forwards again and carry on her journey. She scrabbled to reach for Dad's arms. His fingers closed around her. For one precious moment, they were both suspended together, each holding the other one still against the pull of the time winds.

'What are you doing here?' Dad asked urgently.

Time was short. Noa didn't know everything yet, but she did know that once you stepped into the time tunnel, it was impossible to alter your course. She focused her energy on her dad, and clung with all her might, but the wind was strong.

'I found the key and came looking for you,' she blurted out. There was so much she wanted to tell him, but the wind was starting to howl. 'That doesn't matter now. Where are you going? When are you coming home?'

He flinched, as though the question was an accusation. 'I'm sorry, Noa. I'm so sorry, but I can't come home for a while yet.'

Her chest tightened. She knew she might cry. 'Why not? Please come with me.'

She could feel the irresistible pull of the wind, dragging her towards the Never Door and away from Dad. She gripped tighter.

'I'm searching for your mother.'

Feelings flooded through Noa. She thought of the stained-glass window: the image of her family together, Noa, Dad and Mum, and the message

underneath,
'In Time, We Will
Be Reunited'.
Had she been right?
Could all three of them
be reunited?

'Mum's alive?'
Noa's voice cracked with emotion.

'Yes. I've been tracking time ruptures. There are all kinds of alterations happening, small changes to the fabric of the past. I believe your mum is alive and she's trying to communicate with me, to tell me where and when she is.'

'Changes to fabric?' Noa said, trying to take it in.

'The fabric of the past. Objects where they shouldn't be. Things taken from one time to another. Changes to history that are so tiny, no-one would notice, if they weren't looking closely.'

It was hard to hear Dad over the roaring of the wind. It was relentless now. It took an intense effort to cling on to Dad's arms. 'Will you come back once you've found her?' Noa asked.

Dad looked her right in the eye, holding her as close as he could. 'Noa Goodwin, I will come back to you even if I have to cross oceans and deserts and all of history to do it. I promise.'

Noa relaxed with relief hearing those words, and the wind, exploiting her weakness, finally ripped Dad from her grasp. He was whisked away from her. As he disappeared from view, she heard him call again, 'I promise! I promise!' until he was gone.

Noa and Renwick were buffeted closer to the Never Door, where the wind eased. Noa felt herself washed up against the bottom of the Never Door. 'Are you all right?' she asked Renwick. He nuzzled against her neck for comfort.

Noa looked back at the time tunnel. It carried on as far as she could see, with a million possibilities in every branching path. But she could see no sign of Dad.

She picked herself up, feeling heartsore and bruised. She slipped the key into the Never Door and stepped back into home.